Freight Train
Tren de carga

Donald Crews

Translated from the English by **M. J. Infante**

 Greenwillow Books
An Imprint of HarperCollinsPublishers

rayo

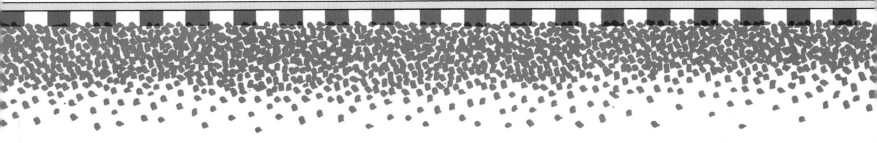

Rayo is an imprint of HarperCollins Publishers.

Freight Train. Copyright © 1978 by Donald Crews. Spanish translation copyright © 2003 by M. J. Infante. All rights reserved. Manufactured in China. No part of this book may be used or reproduced in any manner whatsoever without written permission except in the case of brief quotations embodied in critical articles and reviews. For information address HarperCollins Children's Books, a division of HarperCollins Publishers, 195 Broadway, New York, NY 10007. www.harpercollinschildrens.com

The Library of Congress has cataloged the Greenwillow English-language edition of this title as follows:

Crews, Donald. Freight Train. "Greenwillow Books." Summary: Brief text and illustrations trace the journey of a colorful train as it goes through tunnels, by cities, and over trestles. [1. Railroads—Trains—Pictorial works. 2. Colors. 3. Picture books.] I. Title. PZ7.C8682Fr [E] 78-2303 ISBN 0-688-80165-X (trade bdg.) ISBN 0-688-84165-1 (lib. bdg.) ISBN 0-688-11701-5 (pbk.)

Greenwillow Spanish-English bilingual edition:
ISBN: 978-0-06-056202-1(trade bdg.) ISBN: 978-0-06-056204-5 (pbk.)

First Spanish-English bilingual edition published by Greenwillow Books in 2003.
First Edition 18 19 SCP 20 19 18 17

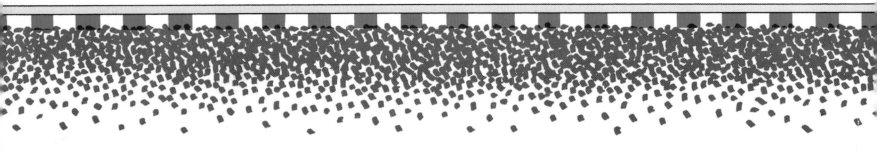

With due respect to Casey Jones, John Henry, The Rock Island Line,
and the countless freight trains passed and passing the big house in Cottondale
Con el respeto debido a Casey Jones, John Henry, The Rock Island Line, y a los trenes de carga
incontables que han pasado y que pasan por la casa grande en Cottondale

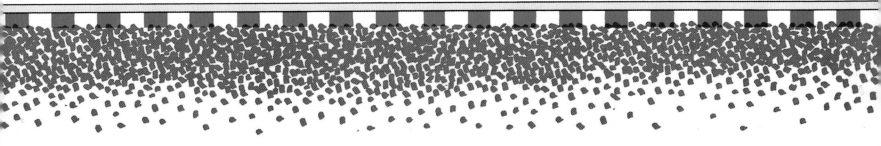

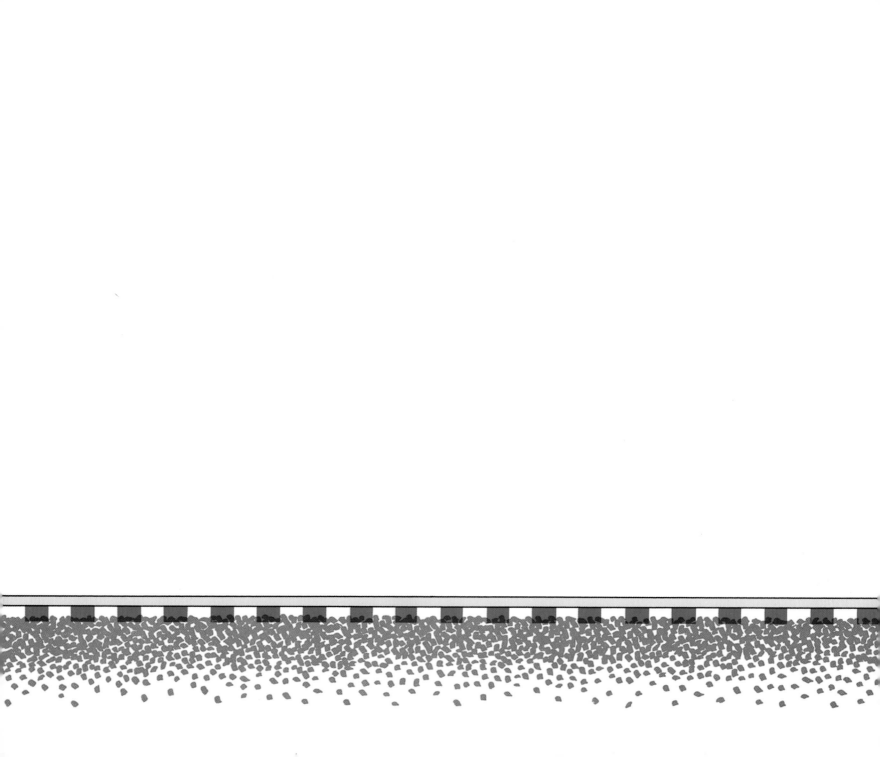

A train runs across this track.
Un tren corre por esta vía.

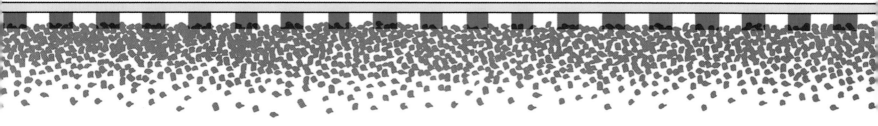

Red
caboose
at
the back

Atrás
el furgón
de
cola rojo

Orange
tank
car
next

**Sigue
un vagón
de tanque
anaranjado**

**Yellow
hopper
car**

**Vagón
de tolva
amarillo**

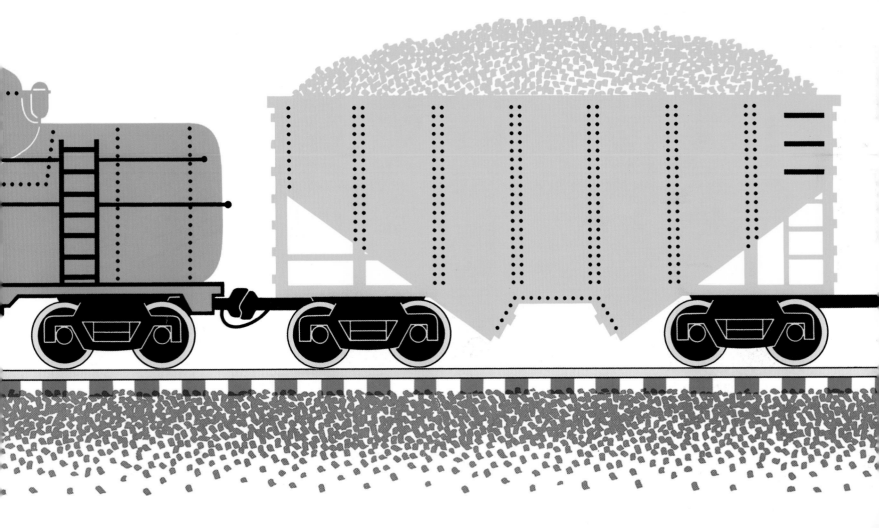

**Green
cattle
car**

**Vagón
de ganado
verde**

**Blue
gondola
car**

Vagón de góndola azul

Purple box car

Vagón morado

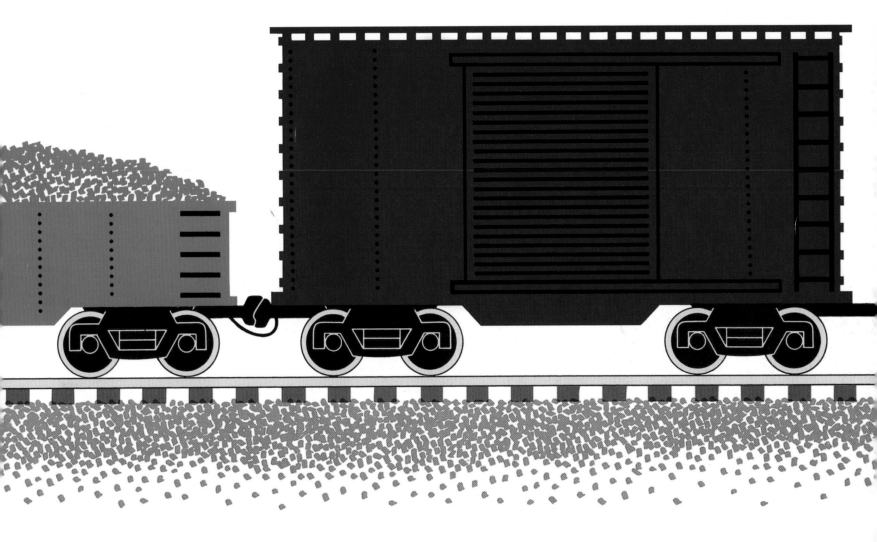

**a Black
tender and**

**un furgón de
ténder negro y**

a Black steam engine.
una locomotora negra.

Freight train.
Tren de carga.

Moving.
Andando.

Going through tunnels
Atravesando túneles

Going by cities
Pasando ciudades

Crossing trestles.
Cruzando puentes de andamio.

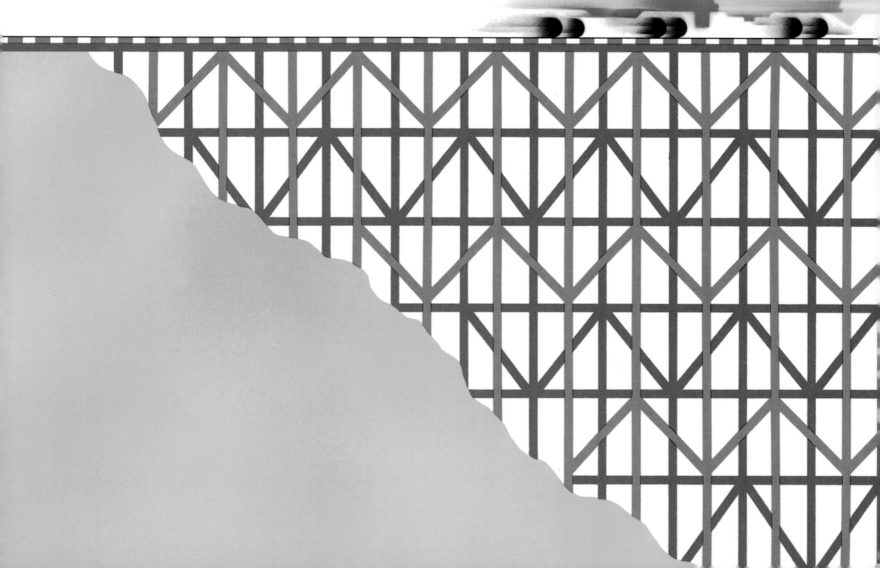

Moving in darkness.
Andando en la oscuridad.

Moving
in daylight.
Going, going...

Andando
en la luz del día.
Se va, se va...

gone.
se fue.